Araminta's

A Magical Opportunity

to Look Within Ourselves

By Charmiene Maxwell-Batten

Copyright

ISBN 978-1-291-35201-6

Second Edition

PRINTED IN UK

Contact:

Charmiene_batten@hotmail.co.uk

http://www.lulu.com/content/13714883

ARAMINTA'S MESSAGE

A Magical Opportunity
to Look Within Ourselves

By Charmiene Maxwell-Batten

Dedication

DEDICATED TO THE COURAGE OF THOSE
WHO SEEK TO REMEMBER
THEIR TRUE HOME.
TO THOSE ALSO,
WHO'S REMEMBRANCE
MAY STILL BE A SEED -
AWAITING THE SUN'S WARMTH.

Books

By Charmiene Maxwell-Batten

My Reflections of America

My Reflections of England

Life, Love and Loss in Switzerland

My Reflections of India and Thailand

My Reflections of Childhood

Reflections of a Housekeeper

A Medley of Musings and Reflections

A Collage of reflections
A Collage of Reflections volume 2

One More Chance

Contents

"All truths are easy to understand,
once they are discovered.
The point is to discover them"

Galileo Gallilei

Acknowledgements

Gratitude to many dear friends from all over the world, all of whom have an eternal place in my heart. Thank you for sharing your heartfulness, sincerity, friendship, honesty and laughter.

DeniseViswanathan, Yolanda Gysler,

Elke von der Osten, Atmo Ram, Brenda Vickery

Jenny Suzumoto, Sina Carroll, Daniel Nirvi Noll,

Daniel Peralta, Lance Fushikoshi, Diana Seropian,

Chinmayo Forro, Marilyn Walls, Karen Young, Darleen

Christopher, Paula Gardiner, Ritzy Ryciak, Kaz Sephton,

…………..and so very many more.

Thank you also to Mira for your editing while we were in Lucknow, India during the winter of 1994\95.

A big thank you to Diana Fairbank for your deeply valued friendship and computer knowledge. Thank you to Laura Redmond and David W. Morin Jr. for your kindness and expert technical skills while I was working with formatting and iBooktores.

Thank you Gabriele Wolf and Timothy Whitmore-Wolf, Deborah Charnes, and Shannon Lacy for allowing me to use some photos that I took on our photo shoots in San Antonio, Texas.

To LeRoy, my husband. Thank you for all the multi-leveled love and support you give me, AND for our lovely garden in Texas!

Six months after this book was first written in 1991, I found myself in Lucknow, India - sitting in Satsang with Sri Poonjaji. This 'knowing' that had arisen from the depths of my spirit and had until now been a soft unidentified whisper, now became a clear voice of truth. The 'whisper' was affirmed.

To Poonjaji, in deep acknowledgement.

Poonjaji died on September 7th 1997

Forward

BY HASAN ASKARI

Fairy tales are more than parables. While a parable requires interpretation in its manifold of meanings preparatory to self-transformation, a fairy tale is alchemy in literary form – as if a magic wand has touched your heart. In their childlike fancifulness fairy tales liberate us from the barrenness of our adult minds, which build sometimes impregnable walls around our soul-center. A fairy tale is the smiling face of one's soul reaching for her liberation as a child looks at a rainbow.

Charmiene gives us a fairy-tale, which is also an allegory at the same time. But the fairy-tale aspect is dominant and hence the artificiality of allegorical construct is subordinated to the felicity of the fairy aspect of the story. Charmiene regards fairies as spirits representing those ideal qualities that humans aspire to. This is in my view the secondary meaning of the symbol. The primary meaning, which the author herself brings out vividly as the story unfolds, concerns that dimension of the fairy world that is resplendent with a sense of unearthly freedom. The author looks at the entire world from flowers to stars as not only governed by

13

inexorable laws but also living the freedom of the Universal Soul, which is represented in the image of the dancing universe.

But for me, Araminta's Message is that of the individual Soul merged in body as if voluntarily to experience the life of the humans, their world and their suffering. In this juxtaposition of two worldviews seen through the same eyes lies the charm and novelty of Charmiene's story. It appears that each one of us is looking at the world from the viewpoint of our formal mind constructs as well as that of a 'fairy' locked within us. One viewpoint covers the other one and it is not through analysis but through an allegory lived as a story that one knows the insider of our being. The discovery of one's Araminta or soul is the tasting of the nectar of freedom.

With ease and tenderness the story moves and recommends itself to imagination and introspection

Hasan Askari, Author and Publisher.
Leeds, *England*
September 1994

Preface

My first book, *Araminta' Message*, seemed to write itself while living on Dartmoor during a cold winter in 1991. Walking through some enchanting woods around Haytor convinced me that fairies gathered and danced amongst the flowers. This inter-dimensional encounter spontaneously inspired me to write about a fairy who came to live in our human world, so that she may communicate the qualities of her inborn realm, while at the same time sharing observations about this corporal world; it was intended as a gift to the human world.

My mother loved the name *Araminta.*

The mystery, innocence and fun experienced by many when reading traditional fairy stories from all over the world, imparts an awareness of the infinite yet uncomplicated wisdom characterized by their nature and their 'world'. These stories are apparently created within the imagination.

Some may already be familiar with the perceptive way in which Marie Louise von Franz has integrated fairy tales and symbols into the workings of human behavior. Many are of course acquainted with the concepts of C. G. Jung, pointing to profound archetypal patterns relating to myths and legends.

Originally written in 1991, Araminta's Message has gone through several revisions. In this book I'm referring to the world of fairies as spirits exhibiting those qualities that perhaps humans struggle for. I sense that people, dwelling in their own self-made prison, are longing to escape this confinement – the invariable question is how?

I have heard that a wise sage approached a man who was clinging fervently to the unyielding bars of a metaphorical prison - as though afraid to let go. Pleading lamentably the man asked the sage: *"How can I be free"*? The sage answered with patience: *"Release the prison bars you are holding, the door is open, you can walk out into freedom"*. The man asked: *"Tell me how to let go of the prison bar that confines me"?*

Certainly it requires particular courage in releasing these allegorical prison bars and the confines that seem so familiar and 'reassuring' to the human mind. A jail that provides a definite sense of security, especially since there is so much camaraderie – many others in that same predicament. Letting go into the unfamiliar and unassuming vastness of liberation is the true and inherent nature of freedom. What a paradox exists on the level of 'mind' understanding. Letting go of obvious bondage would seem a very simple act, yet how deep and fervent is the collective human attachment to this burden. Distorted by fearfulness, bondage appears safer than the unknown and individual path to liberty!

Trees, flowers, sun, moon, rivers, and sky – are all indeed living in freedom. To see a tree dancing its very own and individual dance as the winds sweep by, is for me a spectacle of absolute grace, uniqueness and liberation – a potentiality surely available to us all.

A choice to be happy, free and to be at one with all of life is truly accessible; not always easy – but reachable.

It was only in April 2008, sixteen years after writing this book that I discovered the writings of Dora van Gelder, Elizabeth Ratisseau, Geoffrey Hodson and Walter Evans-Wentz - who have all passed on now. It was quite a revelation to know that they were seeing and feeling what I saw and wrote about in 1991. Having been immersed in childhood fairy tales and mythology from all over the world for as long as I can remember, these time-honored authors struck a chord of unity, recognition and gratitude in me.

Now Araminta will tell you her story!

First Written in 1992

Updated July 1998, Final revision in June 2008

Fairies want humans to be happy and to understand the joy of life.

At one time, fairies openly and heartfully shared their dimension while living in woodlands as nature spirits. They have now moved to another dimension, but have not left us.

Introduction

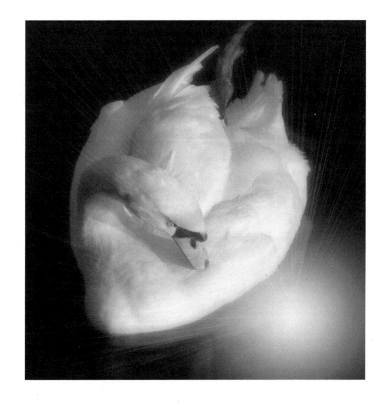

"Imagination is more important than knowledge"

Albert Einstein

"Every man's life is a fairy tale,
written by God's fingers."

Hans Christian Andersen

I'm a fairy living in your world and my name is Araminta – many call me 'Minty'. I volunteered for a special assignment, which involved being born as well as growing up in this human form. A wondrous excitement as well as some apprehension was apparent when this prospect was initially presented. Knowing already certain facets regarding the workings of humankind, I fully realized that it would be a risk; nevertheless the experience of being a physical part of this dimension, motivated a curiosity. Encountering all the difficulties that each and every human faces would undoubtedly be a challenging prospect! I felt ready for it and once it had been agreed, there was no turning back. Being in a human body *has* been a formidable task, sometimes even forgetting why I came - this being one of the known perils to contend with Now that all is remembered, I am eager to unveil some of our secrets and invite you into the world of fairies.

Fairies don't exist on a physical dimension, therefore in one sense we *are* figments of imagination. We're nevertheless very real! Most people don't easily see the non-physical, thus it has been possible to live and visit you by blending easily into nature. When somebody does happen to notice us there seems to be a lot of sensation, debate and great concern in proving it. Our existence on this earth *has* apparently remained somewhat of a mystery.

Due to a natural difference between our two spheres, we had always felt that it was not yet time to communicate through the physical plane. Though recently, the elder fairies looked again at this issue and now feel that both humans and fairies are ready to make contact for our mutual benefit. Consequently, the elder fairies arranged this transition to enter your planet.

Many people now are conscious of the more subtle vibrations and therefore listen with open hearts to the messages from other worlds including my fairy world. Nevertheless, it was considered wise to *send* an actual fairy here for a specific message to be presented and possibly heard. There is a difference in the physics of our two worlds and this manifests in the ability for our dimension to connect with yours through interdimensional travel. There was a time when fairies actually shared physical life in this dimension by living in woodlands as nature spirits – now although the fairies have moved into another dimension they have not left this human realm.

I was told to point out the importance of a communiqué that expresses a desire from the fairy world, to transmit through your verbal language a possible direction towards harmony. We could reveal to you how we live as fairies, so as to present our message as an act of sharing and not as an act of tutoring. We offer this gift of love in the hope of enriching human life. We ourselves have benefited immensely from lessons mastered in human dimension, thus it is with great respect that we offer the physical world an added perspective.

Our Bodies ... Your Bodies

"Dance is a song of the body.
Either of joy or pain."

~Martha Graham

Not being composed of anything physical, fairies seem transparent to the human eye - though sometimes we are mistaken for insects or butterflies. Glimpsing a movement and perhaps a flash or even a multihued throng of colors will indicate and reveal our presence. You may notice the form we wish to make visible - we have been mistaken for butterflies! The shape we project when appearing here in this world is often a disguise and it can be very illusive when being perceived through human eyes. This is our way of playing through the different realms, it's also a safeguard; it would be unwise to expose ourselves without any filters.

To actually see a fairy in the true form without illusion or projection involves a particular approach, best described as 'focusing on emptiness'. This deep relaxation where no thoughts exist is easily found by resting silently amongst flowers, woodlands or along the banks of streams. A little trust is necessary because seeing on another frequency requires practice; it is an unfamiliar skill in this world. By listening on a higher frequency fairies can even be heard singing! Here, this is known as an intuitive approach towards life, which is a mystery and paradox according to 'worldly thinking'. However, an instinctual understanding is gradually becoming accepted in various aspects of tangible science such as quantum physics and the medical field, where vital research is being conducted. Humans have now discovered 'Quantum Entanglement' and this will provide much understanding in the future.

Be cautious, for it's a human characteristic to have harsh expectations when there's a desire to attain goals. An unbending anticipation that something is supposed to happen creates tension and often blocks the very doorway to movement beyond a physical plane, whereas an uncluttered relaxed state of being can and does inspire 'magic'. This is a conceivable perspective with which to transform various aspects of life here on earth.

While being in this human form, numerous unexpected and harsh incidents remind me constantly of mortal and bodily characteristics – there were many challenges to face while adapting. One example of a continuing childhood experience involved bumping into solid things; those were crucial years until finally realizing that solid objects are a glaring reality to the physical form. Walking around them rather than through them seemed and still seems so laborious, but I have no other choice than to respect the reality of a concrete wall.

Initially this body felt slow and burdensome in comparison to a fairy body. I have now learnt patience. Humans can experience gracefulness in spite of the earth's gravity; through persistence and serenity this new and heartening fluidity emerged in my own body, it was a refreshing discovery that resulted in a better understanding of the human form. Deep and resplendent passion has been expressed through pure movement, a truly exquisite language that is beyond any known words.

People exhibit remarkable grace and beauty by being 'in tune' with their physical form; this is particularly evident when performing ballet and Tai chi. When totality is given to these movements, the divine is encountered. Nijinsky, a very great dancer enchanted the public by expressing an apparent disregard towards gravity; he gave his body and soul to the art of dance. Through dedicated passion Nijinsky touched the divine spark of his own soul as well as the soul of all those who saw him dance. He reached beyond the known constricts that can cause limitations in our thinking mind. Humans will come to understand the accessibility of this dynamic in the future.

PAIN

Not having the type of body that is physically hurt, fairies do not experience sensations such as bodily pain. Pain is deeply felt throughout our realm as an internal aching of the spirit; when there is pain for one, it ripples throughout the fairy realm affecting all who are there. It's a shared feeling not an individual one. Pain moves gently away when it's time. We don't try to comfort each other or to stop the pain, nor do we avoid it. We see this phenomenon as part of living so we open our hearts in acceptance to the process, allowing its presence as well as its departure. A fervent denial of pain, or an unbalanced indulgence, causes many humans to misunderstand the process or the journey of pain. Holding onto any emotion or sensation when it's ready to leave, creates more layers of suffering. When sorrow is not fully expressed in the moment of its existence, then it lingers and may fester as a wound. Blame, anger, bitterness may arise from a reluctance to allow anguish a natural pathway towards consciousness. Humans desire control over their emotions, which often creates the reverse effect. Struggling against nature results in a distorted form of expression where one fiercely clings to the idea of restricting, subduing and suppressing emotions. There now exists some concepts for 'New Age' therapists and healers to promise sudden joy and release of pain or grief; this overly and even trendy enthusiasm may not allow for a natural process that is the rightful path for each individual's enlightenment. I've seen marketing ploys presented as books, trainings and workshops during recent years that often give humanity an elusive desire to free themselves from pain. In other words this can be a 'quick fix' which negates a potential seed of growth. Joy and pain are both valuable gifts in this human journey because these vibrational energies reach to the core of our shared universe. It may be wise to understand the profound value of caring, friendship and love so that our pain and our joy are not seen as a lonely journey, but a united resonance.

Pain, embraced in all its honesty and therefore truly accepted, liberates the core of creative expression. Poets and poetry, singers and their songs, writers, dancers, artists come to light! The understanding and release of pain creates compassion. Acceptance - not to be confused with resignation - has been known to release vital energy and an evolvement of consciousness where healing and joy emerge. A natural celebration of life and all it encompasses is felt in the depths of one's spirit. Allowing feelings to be shown in the most vulnerable way may burn away layers of hidden pain. Effort invested in concealing sorrow can then be freed to embrace life in its most ecstatic light.

DIMENSIONS

There are infinite and countless dimensions to be experienced. Due to the nature of our fairy bodies we move through dimensions very easily. By focusing on a certain place we are there in an instant. Achieving such a transition at this moment in human evolution is not possible, although scientists have touched upon a phenomenon called 'time travel' which will eventually enhance the physical comprehension of dimensions. Some people have practiced 'astral travel' enabling them to journey into other areas of vision and knowledge. The human advancement into crossing through dimensions has been hindered by fear of the unknown and a need to follow belief systems fabricated by dubious leaders of politics and other ranks of apparent authority. Emancipation to think freely has been somewhat curtailed by man-made doctrines, intended to control and ensnare the spirit into temporary submission. Movement through dimensions may be hindered until courage overcomes fear, and the spirit is set free to explore the cosmos. There are also countless parallel universes with different physics and mathematics to explain other manifestation of form. Humans may sense the presence of other dimensions, yet it may be confusing and hard to understand within a limited dimensional world.

Fairies prefer to move through dimensions together, in this sense we cannot be described as loners. We have fun moving as a harmonious group; it is an adventure and we're filled with happy thoughts that are easily shared. The movement however does require certain skills so we take care of one another and watch that none gets lost. Our young ones learn this skill gradually, never taking it for granted. As our life span continues this art becomes more refined and requires great awareness. It may seem easy because we have developed the skills over time; the ability develops and matures as wisdom grows, which is appropriate. There exists great harmony when knowledge and true wisdom move at an equal pace. It is questionable whether this has occurred on the earth realm where science and technology have advanced with speed and the balancing factor of wisdom as well as awareness may not have progressed with a matching speed. Thus a resulting imbalance transpires, leading to a narrow perspective where greed and self-interest are deceptive focal points.

TEMPERATURE

Fairies perceive the sensation of temperature quite differently than humans. Oh, how often I have ignored this human body when white, crispy clean snow was gently falling in flakes outside my window - my only thought was to play and sink into the soft feathery bed of fluff with no notion of temperature. After shivering and shaking with cold, the realization came yet again that I now have a body to consider. The concept of protecting our fairy body with raincoats, overcoats, umbrellas, bikinis, sun tan oil, simply does not exist. We are aware of sun, snow, beaches and ocean as a non-physical sensation and our experience of it is full and complete. To deal with the paraphernalia required in adorning and protecting the human body felt cumbersome to me.

Now, even in this more encumbered yet cherished human form I continue to recognize the elements of nature with all the joy and vitality of my fairy soul. An unexpected and blissful discovery happened one day when my physical form and my heart was filled with exuberance; it was a discovery that pointed me in a direction where I could see the physical body not as a burden, but as an instrument of learning. The realization of a soul's capacity in reaching out to the physical body will also depend on the level of freedom from a reasoning intellect. It is better to embrace the pure experience in that very moment, rather than allowing the logical mind to intrude, thereby freezing an event so that a 'photograph' or imprint on the brain is all that is left to seize and ponder on. However this imprint in the brain's memory connections has great value in some circumstances.

FOOD AND EATING

Actually we don't eat. The closest we come to that is drinking nectar from flowers just like hummingbirds. It is delicious and a little goes a long way. Fairies are accustomed to absorbing their nourishment in the form of sunshine, air, rain, mist and best of all is the scent of flowers. A human body is designed to inhale the scent of a flower as pure pleasure, whereas the fairy being is replenished in every way by the fragrance. Nature, seen as beauty to the human eye is our food and sustenance. My human body would stop functioning with a fairy diet, but my inner soul remains deeply and fervently replenished by it.

I have maintained certain agility on this physical plane by eating clean light food. Light and natural food gives me a feeling of enthusiasm within this physical form, heavy foods filled with unnatural ingredients will weigh me down and transform my body into a prison. It's a horrible sensation!

Eating was an interesting process to learn here, it seemed to be a laborious and necessary task that required great effort at first. Now that I eat small portions of delectable food, I can appreciate the joys of having an appetite. I do continue to eat extremely slowly – some things can't be changed in such a short time!

COMMUNICATION

Being exposed to the human language was initially a shock to me. Loud noises thrown at one another across rooms; mouths contorted into different shapes – I felt dazed by it. During my time here I have come across many humans who speak in gentle tones, which is much easier for me to listen to.

Whenever I feel assaulted by booming noises, I quietly move away from the source of it, and then I am not so shell-shocked. After being in a crowded place with blaring sounds I usually seek out the flowers, who speak in soft whispers. Once I am amongst my friends, the flowers, I feel revived again.

Sometimes I wonder whether humans really want to be talking as much as they do; are many forcing this just to be polite?

Has verbal expression been misused or misunderstood? Has it been manipulated to hide true feelings? I wonder about these matters. I love hearing voices expressed in musical singing. Through this heavenly medium one can touch higher levels that are outside the physical realm. When singing voices exude such exquisite beauty, the caressing sound reaches beyond this world and far out to other worlds where it is felt and reciprocated.

Being much attuned to one's dog or cat or horse – within seconds a feeling can be conveyed without the lengthy structures of words. A mother will often hear what her baby is saying, as her heart lovingly and quietly listens. There is little chance of misinterpretation in this form of communication, as long as the heart is open and the skeptical mind doesn't interfere with the transmission. Direct contact in this form is remarkably clear, more so than the often-awkward attempts at verbal explanations.

Poems and poetry will undoubtedly impart the exceptional beauty of a feeling or an event by conveying art, through words. I believe some poets have an ability to free themselves by allowing their passion to take life in the form of written words - the poet's heart remains unshackled. I have been moved to tears by the simplicity and poignancy of Japanese Haikus':

OH! Moon so golden bright.

Even the birds are fooled

And sing their dawn songs

Haiku by Atmo Ram

Children

"If you want your children to be brilliant,
read them fairy tales.
If you want them to be geniuses,
read them more fairy tales."

~Albert Einstein

Voiced effortlessly and filled with spontaneity, children begin life without self-imposed censorship; characteristics that in later life may be lost altogether and become a deep longing instead.

Innocence in human children is a gift at birth that serves to align their body and soul in purity and non-duality. Once they have learnt to be 'political' or to hide their truth, a natural innocence fades and the double-edged apple of knowledge is eaten. A precious jewel that came so easily in childhood becomes mankind's shared soul-journey through a worldly manifestation of seeking and the innermost yearning to re-discover that precious diamond.

A lifestyle not attuned to openness or authenticity can prepare children to hide behind a façade, to say only what they 'should' say. Discontent and neurosis develop through unnatural behavior and therapists pop up to fulfill the demand for healing. Recognizing the wisdom of an original childlike nature once it is forfeited, may not be so easy to unearth again. It becomes a testing path of discovery.

Although puzzled by the conduct of adults, children soon learn to adapt – willingly or unwillingly. They may also rebel against this forced code of behavior and by being deemed disobedient or in need of discipline their cry for acceptance is ignored.

The song by Pink Floyd, 'One more brick in the wall', was maybe a cry for freedom for those children who wish to grow into who they are and not to become just another brick in a wall. Nature created us as a seed to blossom into adulthood, each in our own unique way, which is a mystery until it happens. We may not know in advance how our life will reveal itself. Humans seem to be afraid of mysteries; allowing each moment to unfold is often an unfamiliar and alarming affair or an upsetting ordeal! There is a tendency to panic and cling on to concepts, limitations and so-called security, which could be an illusory idea of safety.

Fairies love earth children. No hard protective shell surrounds the younger or happier children because natural receptivity is present in a remarkable way. Earth children are typically playful, loving and candid, they are *themselves,* and they are *real.* In an atmosphere of mutual authenticity, communication becomes very clear. Adults who have retained a conscious vulnerability are frequently known to be sages and teachers of higher wisdom. Conscious vulnerability is a strength that is so deep, I compare it to a willow tree blowing wildly about in stormy weather – bending with supple ease and surrender as the gusts roar by – yet not breaking. 'Stronger' and unbending trees are more likely to break when forceful blustery weather assails them.

> *"Nothing is as strong as gentleness;*
> *nothing as gentle as real strength"*
> St. Francis de Sales

People certainly appear fearful of embracing their own receptivity and tenderness. Seeing it as weakness or naivety, they often believe it necessary to sustain an appearance of restrain while deluding themselves and others in this forced attempt to hide their 'weaknesses. Self-protective and hostile barriers are erected in order to shield that seemingly fragile and susceptible place in your heart. I am not surprised to see that actual weapons have been and are being built! Could this be an outer manifestation of inner anxiety?

Despite so much fear and defense there prevails a sincere and immeasurable longing for mutual friendship.

Children with their innate ability are constantly demonstrating to adults, ways in which to be playful and to be themselves once again. It may be more helpful to learn from children than visiting the therapist. Children haven't learnt to hold back and therefore are not exposed to the dangers of excessive control. Expressing themselves with delight and tremendous emancipation is a joy to behold. When inspired by music they will simply dance or sing or both! It reminds me of birds flying through the air and singing their morning songs. In fact it is reminiscent of the intrinsic flow of nature, dancing with life.

Stress and anxiety seem to take over the human body when life becomes too *serious*; I have certainly felt this in my own human body. I am not advocating a denial of our burdens or challenges in the course of a lifetime, but I myself prefer to use a different word. The word I prefer to use is *sincerity*. Sincerity does not imply avoidance of responsibility; it simply suggests dealing with a situation without the tension and anxiety that humans are so attached to. Playing with a child demonstrates how *sincerity* can be far more harmonious and yes relaxing, than *seriousness*.

Children in the fairy dimension are 'the young ones'. The concept of age is very different where one has a physical form. A fairy body does not age in the same way that a human body does. In our world, age becomes wisdom and it is only on reaching maturity, that we are sent to communicate with the elders of other dimensions.

Our young ones are free to move about as they wish – except through dimensions. They need to learn specific procedures and of course a valuable quality of wisdom is required before embarking on this development. We teach our young ones some practical skills, one of which is to move through dimensions with adeptness.

Our young ones are taught to play gently with insects and flowers, they are taught important communication skills with all of life's creation. We do not teach them to hide who they are; to pretend they are different than who they are or to reject their very existence. As pure beings, all originate from the greatest mystery; we are compelled therefore to respect that creation and would not wish to criticize our own existence nor the existence of others. Self-destructive behavior seems to originate from self-rejection, and a deep condemnation for even being alive torments those who cannot accept themselves for who they are. Eating disorders and addictions seem to have a connection with self-hatred. Reproaching our very own creation would seem as harsh as rebuking a flower or tree for their existence. Since being in this human form I see the doubts and judgments that people thrust upon themselves as well as others around them. This not only causes distress but it distracts from living full and vital lives.

The concept of ownership does not exist with our fairy children. This is different in the human realm where each child belongs to a set of parents, or else the child is abandoned or orphaned and then housed in community home for children; those children often feel that they 'do not belong anywhere'. A child growing up with a regular set of parents fits the predominating structure here in this world, a structure that is considered 'normal' even though other attempts at child rearing have been explored. A few people have found their answers by raising children in communes; some of those children appear to have grown into relaxed adults and their sociable interactions seem more authentic. Children who have been insulated with their parents may grow up to be shy or ill at ease with others. For numerous grown-ups on this plane, mixing with other people seems to require great effort, frequently dealt with by a façade of polite talking. After which they run off to a separate and sometimes lonely spot to recuperate.

Being alone can be very beautiful, an exquisite way to feel the depth of silence without feeling lonely. Humans living alone or as a group or even a family, are sometimes unable to relate or respond to others in a comfortable and restful way. They can be in a group and feel lonely; they can be alone and still feel lonely. People here can be very lonely. A child on the other hand, not yet manipulated or damaged by a structure may be alone – but not lonely! They are absorbed totally in the present moment, feeling

44

content. The disruptive and limited thought of loneliness does not enter their mind, nor does it enter the room, therefore loneliness itself is not an issue. Fairies do not spend time alone to hide or escape, we love being together as much as being alone. It is just another color in life's rainbow.

There are two different perceptions of solitude, in the same way that there are two sides of fear. A clear demonstration of the differences becomes apparent as you observe children growing up. *Fear* can be instinctive when a naturally healthy panic arises and adrenalin surges purposefully around the body – there's a need to run fast when you notice a grouchy bull in a field nearby! The other type of fear is programmed into children at a young age - a pointless and futile sensation of dread, creating anxiety and sleeplessness and even magnifying into larger-than-life proportions. In the same way loneliness can be an authentic emotion that is expressed with an open and loving heart, or it can be a thought pattern that simply creates havoc by sabotaging your enjoyment of being by yourself. People can even become self-piteous and think themselves a victim of loneliness, *or* they can enjoy it as children often do. It is a choice!

The silence of a flower garden and the silence of a graveyard clearly demonstrate how one is vibrant with life and the other, dead. Though in all respect to those who hold tender memories, shedding their tears by the graveside of one they have loved and still love –

they certainly bring the fragrance of a flower garden by their heartfelt tears of love.

The qualities of silence can indeed be brimming and radiant, or barren and bleak. Being alone can feel vibrantly alive, soothingly quiet – or it can be desolate. I think it is a matter of releasing the overtones of fear, control and negativity.

Children may possibly be taken for granted; I've seen in some situations where people produce a child as proof they are 'like everyone else' or to bolster their image. These motives often result in neglect on various levels, towards a child. Children are very precious and my deep belief is that much can be learned by being attentive to them as well as guiding them through the initial years of their introduction to a curious and new planet. The wisdom of pure innocence, truth, laughter and trust is not only vital to these little ones, but is truly rewarding to their guardians. Take time to hear the wisdom that embodies each child because children see truth beyond a façade. Even though they have not mastered the worldly terminology to verbalize it, they *do* express wisdom in a far higher realm than the limited form of words can articulate. Many adults have recently traveled to the East in search of innermost truth, the living essence of which is on their doorstep, revealed daily by thousands of children.

I see in children the quality of celebration so much sought after, perhaps unconsciously by adults seeking to heal themselves, seeking to feel alive, searching for innermost peace.

"Follow your bliss
and the universe will open doors
where there were only walls"

Joseph Campbell

Relaxation

"Nothing can be truer than fairy wisdom.
It is as true as sunbeams."

Douglas William Jerrold

There are some profound differences between our two worlds here - let me elucidate by saying that in this material dimension, the earth, water, sun and air can provide a spontaneous link to a higher frequency of consciousness *and* the non-physical dimension. In human form, we revitalize ourselves by swimming in salty azure seawater or a transparently clear lake and playing in the waves or stretching out on a warm beach with the sun gently nurturing our body. Walking through woodlands, along the banks of streams or up into the purely invigorating mountains peaks will bring immeasurable relief and a state of well-being to the body and psyche. This very state of *being* allows wisdom to enter our consciousness. By creating this 'open door', vital insights touch upon the deepest levels of awareness. This often occurs in a state of relaxation.

Some may think of relaxation as being lazy, even characterizing it as indolence while finding it difficult to sanction in themselves or others. Those who can't truly relax will formulate a disapproving and sometimes embittered outlook. Others may prove this judgment to be a justified likelihood by living a lifestyle of self-abuse and lethargy; a heavy spirit cannot be content. Relaxation and sluggishness may on the surface appear quite similar; in reality the two very differing attitudes are worlds apart.

Alertness, clarity, awareness and peace are attained through genuine relaxation. Languishing with unabashed ease, a cat sleeps peacefully with no sign of tension. If a noise arises the cat is immediately alert and ready. Relaxation is so total that in turn he can be completely alert and present. Living naturally that cat does not suffer anxiety or insomnia; his energy is not dissipated therefore he really can relax. When sleep time is disturbed by anxiety, the time to be alert will also be disturbed by weariness from the night before. Many people panic and swallow tablets to force sleep; I believe that an answer to this dilemma may be found in other ways. Relaxation is a forgotten art, which really can be re-learnt and practiced. Great rewards are discovered through this revival. Since this state of being is maintained inherently in the fairy world, it was a shock to feel so much tension permeating my human body when I first arrived here; what a relief to discover soothing techniques, which dissolve the stress. Try languishing in a warm and calming bath – I did. Floating around in the cool clear water also reminds me of my fairy world; I find myself letting go of tension while experiencing serene comfort. Blissful memories come flooding back to me, while washing away any heaviness that accumulated.

Humans have recently discovered a new way of giving birth in water, sometimes with dolphins as midwives. The newly born babies love this! Entering the solid world from the safe and fluid womb of their mother is often a harsh ordeal and a shock, but entering the world through water has proved to be a gentler approach for those young ones. Water imparts a quality of healing to the human body, not only absorbing tension but even allowing it to dissipate - one is cleansed on many levels. When humans are grumbling or fighting with one another, stress is passed around as though it were flu; it cannot be flushed out while continually being thrown from one person to another. Allowing tension to melt away is a conscious approach that can inspire a harmonious and nurturing environment for everyone.

As speedy lifestyles become more prominent on this planet, pressure and anxiety accumulate without warning. Other than changing the structure, it would be helpful for individuals to be more aware of the effects of negative actions. I have seen humans forcing their physical bodies beyond all healthy boundaries without even realizing it. In order to gain better health people have begun to 'work out', jog and exercise as an active form of relaxation - exhilarated faces are noticeable during and after exercising. We all love to see the freshly content facial expressions after all this dynamic activity! Facial expressions are miraculously transformed in a relaxed and playful body; those rigid hard lines on the forehead disappear and the tight fearful lips are replaced by an expression of animated receptivity. Children exercise their bodies while thoroughly enjoying themselves - playfully running, skipping, jumping. They look and feel happy! Ironically, facial expressions may also become taut especially when exercising is taken too seriously. A paradox! The determined and *anxious* drive to work out in order to relax is a contradiction that reminds me of our numerous conflicts in life. Some have already noticed an intrinsic connection between physical and mental health when they can rest and enjoy themselves.

Relaxation may be hard to find in this modern human world for there exists a structure involving driving ambitions, which have become obsessive. One problematic aspect of this goal orientated structure is a defiant tendency to 'break out of it' in various ways. One enticing yet deceptive way for some to 'break free' is through the temporary gratification provided by drugs. Certain drugs that trigger 'happy sensations' are a short-lived illusion of freedom and a momentary escape from the burden of a troubled mind. It is sadly clear that a desperate need to relax without the understanding of how to attain it generates a frantic need to take flight, in whatever way opens up! Since many on this planet are ardently seeking solutions, a glimpse at something different may be all that is needed to regain harmony.

Every living being seeks to live in unity as well as the freedom to express their own unique spirit. For those who are longing to see through and beyond any limitation, the fairy world and other realms too, can share and offer a window towards the threshold of limitless possibility.

"There will always be faeries and elves within nature because they will always be dancing within our hearts."

~Ted Andrews

Playing

"*Wherever you go,*
spread Life, playfulness and joy
to every corner of the earth"

Osho

"On with the dance!

Let joy be unconfined...

- Byron

Playfulness is an important part of fairy existence and our reality. We enjoy crossing into this earth dimension where children almost always notice us. Fairies can make things seem invisible, and then visible again; if you notice something vanishing and materializing once more, a few young fairies are sure to be playing with some objects. No harm or mischief is meant, it's simply that they enjoy using their newly learnt skills at an early age, just like earth children enjoy learning to walk and speak. Merrymaking through dimensions is always an enthralling venture for young fairies.

When fairies are having fun on this earth plane, humans are spontaneously pervaded with lighthearted feelings and will instinctively want to laugh and enjoy life. This is an effect of having fairies close by! In summertime surrounded by the natural beauty of nature, it is much easier for the body to relax into playfulness - picnics are a good opportunity for this.

In winter where the magnificence of mountains against a clear blue sky provokes extraordinarily deep felt emotions and moments of inspiration, we fairies celebrate an ensuing intimacy between our two worlds where the earth and fairy realm are diffused in unity. In such times of rest, vibrancy of life enters the psyche, tremendous release occurs and this is the open door that allows expansion to flow into the spirit, unimpeded by the reasoning mind. When feeling lonely without fairy friends, in spite of a human form I still try to connect with them because the longing for effortless and loving laughter is a beautiful memory from long ago. It's not easy to maintain this cherished contact in a closed environment, yet in nature the bridge between these two worlds is visibly accessible. Hearing sounds from the fairy world comes first and then I vaguely see them; my human eyes are not as sharp as fairy vision, and human ears often muffle the sounds. Alertness is now vital in order to maintain an inherent clarity of these higher frequency senses.

Playing enables relaxation to exist, relaxation inspires playfulness, a new dawn arises and fresh life pours in, allowing the glimpse of unforgettable bliss, which ignites and empowers the unique path of every being.

How about work and survival amongst all this playful relaxation you may ask? Well this is the magic! Abundance flows through the very sources that have been freed, life begins to flow with you and you begin to flow with life. The sad but familiar act of grasping – originating from fear and greed, will seem pointless. Only when the flow of life seems to be passing you by and you feel disconnected with the pulse of life's heartbeat, does the act of grasping become so apparently crucial.

Fairies really love playing with children because their sight is still so pure. They can see us. They haven't learnt to verbalize this recognition so it remains a secret - unrevealed. Since adults have almost, but not totally forgotten the ability to acknowledge life beyond the physical, this gift in their children may go unnoticed. Even now as a human adult, I still find joy and delight when playing with children. When children are near me I fall into a familiar sense of ease, playfulness and laughter for which I am truly grateful.

I recall an afternoon while standing quietly at a bus stop fully absorbed in an inner sadness and feeling a bleak weariness of the human world, when suddenly I looked up to see a pair of kind brown kind eyes glancing and then smiling at me. It was so heartening. This young teenage girl glowed with compassion through all the noise and chaos of the world. I saw the pure energy of sensitivity and it elevated my spirit once again. This event is inexplicable, except that fairy friends may have been present at that moment. Or perhaps more fairies have arrived on this earth since my own entry. Although the answer to this is unknown in my present state, the warmth of friendship and understanding was clearly visible.

I love reading children's stories; intertwined with dreaminess one becomes engrossed in the enchantment and messages of uncomplicated truth. When watching an animated film titled 'The Last Unicorn', a young unicorn had taken on a human form and I recognized my own predicament. The film characterized a unicorn who changed into human shape for a specific reason, and she too felt the weight of her new form as soon as she transformed into the mortal body of a woman.

It seems so very long ago when entering this world with my friends while still in the energy of a different dimension. I wonder when I will see them all again with all the clarity and simplicity that I had known before.

WATERFALLS

I love waterfalls! If you come across these dynamic, sparkling, gushing, flowing, cascading curtains of water on your walks, it is likely there will be lots of fairies around. By sitting quietly and allowing the timeless emptiness of the moment to unfold, you will feel and perhaps hear their laughter. Fairies delight in this contact; it is a bridge between our two worlds. Another universe can be touched.

Fairies are passionate about lakes and streams but waterfalls are our favorite; dancing beneath them is to be showered in light and colors. Fairies are not affected by temperature or by the pressure of down pouring water because it feels like music and illumination falling upon us. Although this is a less cumbersome state than the human body is accustomed to, I believe that the human body is able to achieve this very lightness. By embracing wholeness, many have already found their way to a sense of emancipation from corporal weightiness, while still maintaining their awareness of being in a physical world. Any attempts at avoiding or denying the physical solidity causes a struggle, whereas denying nothing is to be whole and complete – is to be truly free. It is through the physical that humans can attain the non-physical. I am speaking as one who faces the same challenges that all humans confront. Although my message is one of optimism, my journey in this body involves the whole spectrum of mortal and painful challenges.

DRUGS

While I happily noticed the vivacity of those who indulged in various forms of heightened and alternate realities through what is known as pleasurable drugs, the ambiguous circumstances were apparent when the laughter and amusement was short lived because it was synthetically produced. Induced playfulness is very temporary. Sadly and ultimately it also causes damage to the physical body as well as the psyche.

There are other ways to achieve a lightness of spirit within this physical form, the outcome of which is greater strength and health to the human body. There are other and more sustaining ways to experience heightened awareness. Since fairies can't attach themselves to a physical form, the idea of using chemicals in this way would not present itself as it has done here. This dilemma and the resulting anguish on this planet is an enigma. Perhaps the use of recreational drugs is a daring attempt to reach freedom beyond the limitations of a worldly structure.

Native American Indian culture, with great foresight and knowledge, focused on the use of plants to attain visions of insight. With a long established civilization involving specific rituals handed down through generations and designed to strengthen their understanding, they incorporated strict preparations for the body and psyche before embarking on this powerful journey. A journey that was to direct them into deeper knowledge and a 'doorway' into a new awakening. Plants and hallucinogenic drugs were utilized as a discipline where ensuing visions were honored and respected. Humans carelessly using drugs may experience haphazard hallucinations; those with weaker and more vulnerable personalities experience gaps in their psyche. Gaps that have been opened too hastily, like unripe fruit picked before being ready. The fissures often become wounds to the inner health and state of mind.

Often regarded as irresponsible or frivolous, playfulness has been discarded and even criticized. Playfulness like relaxation seems for many, difficult to attain, even though it requires no effort. I think it has been forgotten through the years of growing up.

Watching dolphins surfing through the ocean has given us all such tremendous joy, as wordless vibrations permeate the human heart and playfulness stirs afresh within our spirit. I find myself remembering moments of timeless hours of diving, jumping and rolling over boisterous white-capped waves on the Island of Hawaii. This is a natural 'high', giving life to body and soul. Dolphins are great teachers in this mortal world. They can teach us and reach us with the gift of heightened awareness.

Playfulness is a precious quality of life - an attribute through which many have discovered deep and startling emotional healing. To the human mind it may seem worthless and even superficial. It is not worthless as has now been scientifically proven that all body cells respond positively to laughter and relaxation; people do recover from ill health in this way.

The art of living joyfully is truly a sincere path towards illumination, health and a way to regenerate this beautiful planet.

"We Only grow old
when we stop
playing"

George Bernard Shaw

Flowers

" A flower cannot blossom

without sunshine,

and man cannot live without love"

Max Muller

Flowers are intrinsic to the lives of fairies - both live within many planes of existence. Fairies feel a natural camaraderie with their floral family.

In the non-earth dimension, flowers express melodic sounds as well as their gorgeous scents and distinctive colors. Fairies receive nourishment and sustenance from merging with the beauty of nature; each deep breath while inhaling the fragrance of a rose or a lily and each glance at a bright flowery color, is life giving. Without nature, our senses would starve and we would waste away.

Even in this body an attachment to flowers has never ceased. I still feel nourished by each breath of perfume and every burst of color, which are all as unique and vibrant as are their myriad forms.

Light hearted and graceful beings, flowers are cherished friends and that's why at one time, it upset me so much to see them being ruthlessly cut and taken into concrete buildings to die; when trying to reach out and rescue them, knowing that their physical life had been severed, I had misunderstood a meaningful gesture. Though the misapprehension occurred earlier in my childhood years, an awareness of how dissimilar conditions may cause judgments and even condemnation of others with differing views was evident.

Situations are often seen from alternate perspectives and a true recognition of this impasse can bring about expansion and compassion rather than disapproval. People were placing flowers in their living space with the same affection that I myself felt and feel – love for their colors, scents and sheer presence in a room. The therapeutic effect of flowers can help to alleviate depression; joy and healing take place when people have flowers in their home.

It is a happy vision to see people tending their gardens, and expressing affectionate triumph at the beautiful roses nurtured into bloom. Honeysuckle tenderly encouraged into climbing archways; lilac trees bending gracefully with their load of fragrant blossom - yes many people in this dimension love and treasure flowers.

In our world, flowers impart great wisdom. When we fail to see clearly, they are there for us, silently sharing important insights. As we sing, their delicate murmuring sounds join our tunes. When we dance, they sway with elegance as the breeze frolics by. Listening to the silence of flowers and hearing their murmuring whispers soon dispels the assumption that wisdom can only be verbalized through words.

Flowers resonate on a high frequency which reminds me of my own world; it is sound and motion that can't always be received by earthly senses, because the eyes and the ears of humans may not have the capacity to tune into the pitch of this frequency. I sense a yearning in humans to be closer to flowers, to trees and nature itself and to regain a long forgotten language of stillness. Many have already found that a slight adjustment in their outlook may be all that is needed to regain this language.

The gift imparted by flowers can be compared to unconditional love. Being aware of this remarkable gift, we compare it to the possibility of total love in the earthly world. Many humans who sense this potentiality are now reaching out with courage and desire to establish ways to live with kindness in their heart. Forgiveness also brings a deeper understanding to the flow of life as well as an inspired love of the earth, which prompts an empathetic willingness not to pre-judge or rebuke others.

Flowers die in this dimension, death being the nature of all things in a physical world. Before moving into this earth realm they foresee and understand the outcome of physical life; nevertheless they are willing to come here because their short life brings so much joy and hope to mankind. Though the concept of dying is a natural occurrence in a material world, this compelling issue is seen very differently from other planes of existence.

"The Temple bell stops,
but I hear the sound coming out of the flowers"

~ Basho

Love

"Lovers don't finally meet somewhere,
they're in each other all along"

Rumi

"Life without love
is like a tree without blossoms or fruit"

Kahlil Gibran

Being in love, the music of euphoria within your heart translates into vitality and you feel beautiful. The paradise of romantic and heightened joy reveals a similarity with our two worlds, where both dimensions experience a merging of energy integrating as a union of love. When two beings chance upon an attraction, a magnetism of tenderness and sensuality combine into an exquisite dance - a synthesis of color and light. Yes - our young ones emerge from this union too!

It's a specially purposeful and conscious fusion and there are *no* accidents. Once we have bonded with another luminosity we carry a part of the other's radiance with us through eternity. When you are in love and you blend with another spirit, you embrace a part of that person always - love *is* eternal.

Humans on this planet have experienced physical and spiritual love in its joyous entirety. As you merge with others, each of these lights is carried within yourself. Here on this earth plane one can gently touch the hand of someone you love and a merging of energies occurs from this simple and conscious contact. The ocean-like electro-magnetic field that surrounds and transports energy, connects our consciousness to others and as evolution develops this can become a positive strength for humanity's transformation and awakening.

I would like to mention the institution of marriage as identified here on this planet. The most common concept is of a man and a woman partnered for life through a beautiful and sanctified ritual of vows. It is a valuable as well as practical concept that has also proved controversial, as too have alternate structures of marriage where a man may have many wives. The functional issues around the marriage structure involves an optimistic and prudent approach to child rearing; another beneficial aspect of the joint household is companionship and support to better sustain the task of living in an ordered society where there are shared goals to attain. The cherished and tender side of the marriage agreement begins and results in a sincere deepening of love. I have seen infinitely bright love between two elderly people in their eightieth year, after spending a lifetime together - knowing that they have walked a path of courage and love, hand-in-hand. Whereas two people who optimistically enter into marriage, may unexpectedly grow in different directions. Fresh young love inspires growth like the warmth of sunshine inspires a tree to grow green and strong; but it can be nothing but stifling when two people have matured to full potential in totally different ways and yet forcibly remain in the marriage structure - for the wrong reasons.

You might possibly divorce and split up in this realm. The original burning flame of love becomes the instantly recognizable love of warm friendship - in an ideal situation; love never disappears it just changes form. Or after a few years of marriage, you may not even remember the fire of joy that brought you together in the first place; forgotten or else modified, the original spark may become dull and tiresome in some relationships – perhaps the challenges of living together were too great. People sometimes become angry and resentful when things change - there are some unpleasant divorces here! Blame and criticism is thrown around, due to rigid expectations of one's partner's role or else unyielding resistances to fine-tuning the bond you have together – there are numerous scenarios for the prolongation of culpability. Change can be painful. The concept of monogamy can cause confusion here. Monogamy, a beautiful dynamic, has been sadly linked with unbending control and negativity. When dominance and manipulation are incorporated in the 'agreement' of relationship, there are harsh repercussions.

I can't think of any universal rules that apply to all situations where marriage and relationship are concerned. The simple truth is that each person has to follow his or her own sense of authenticity and become *aware* when fear or pain turns into anger and resentment. Fairies live in monogamy because it is simply a deepening of love without the painful turmoil of earthly emotions interfering in the bond of affection. When I see swans here on earth, floating along the water in pairs, I am reminded of the natural bond of love in my fairy world.

Mankind seems burdened by fear of abandonment, which can sabotage the understanding of trust. In the human world there are great challenges as a relationship grows and moves through deeper layers of time and consciousness. It is a delicate and individual decision whether or not to move through the layers *together*, or else to move through them alone. Whatever the choices being made, it will not be helpful to incorporate negative passion.

The fairy world does not relate to emotions of jealousy and possessiveness, they have no manifestation in our dimension. Though as a human, these emotions have arisen and in those moments I've tried to make a choice - an option *not* to take delivery of them has proved to be valuable. In other words it is better to let these sensations arise and move on without giving them any further possibility to expand and destroy love.

Sensuality here is often linked with vigorous physical contact, an activity that is labeled as 'good sex'. I see no problem with the passionate and spirited union of two bodies, but when the physical activity is lacking any heart, it is devoid of life and even

78

becomes an aggressive attempt to get 'high'. As in drug use, one is never fulfilled by an empty illusion - while true ecstasy is profoundly meaningful and genuinely uplifting.

By quietly lying beside each other and breathing together, you will connect with a universal love; the energy of sensuality emerges as a divine dance, without being forced or manipulated. The ancient art of tantric love has been known to transform sexual pulsation into a flowing force of vitality; the 'electrical current' of a naturally emerging sensuality surges through your body like a flowing river that rejuvenates cellular function while bringing life, healing and health into the body and mind.

Humans' desire to be in total command of their lives even though the very character of sensuality cannot be controlled - it arises and is set in motion through blissful relaxation. Trusting your body to feel and enjoy the moment without any goal to attain creates a magical and nameless experience. By simply lying on some grass and gazing into the sky, you will find your spirit dancing with the flow of nature itself. It's not an action to do it is a place to be. Floating in water, sitting amongst flowers, running through fields – will ignite the joy of innocence as the dance of your body and souls unite in complete harmony.

The human mind has attempted to form constricts and concepts around the sensation of love and sensuality - an attempt which may limit the unique and spontaneous spark of life. Love is bliss, and love is pain - moving through bliss or pain with awareness, grace and acceptance is the ultimate path, not the goal. The mortal mind has not been created to comprehend the vast spark of ultimate and spiritual 'purpose', whereas it is easily understood, when stepping beyond the mind and into your heart.

Celebrate love, why try to capture it?

"Dance is the hidden language of the soul."

~Martha Graham

Trees and Rocks

"Trees are sanctuaries.

Whoever knows how to speak to them,

Whoever knows how to listen to them,

Can learn the truth.

They do not preach learning and precepts.

They preach the ancient law of life"

Herman Hesse

With deep echoing voices and resonating on a parallel frequency as rocks - trees are powerful and wise elders. Fairies have the utmost respect for these ancient beings, whose intelligence extends far beyond the comprehension of an exclusively reasoning mind. Receiving the wisdom they offer, requires presence and awareness; trees and rocks hold nothing back, it is left to anyone to hear and see for him or herself. The druids here in olden times, understood and recognized the significance of this knowledge and

Intellect on this plane has had extreme and almost exclusive relevance attached to it and since it does require manifestations of proof, a pathway of vision on various other levels may have been blocked. Proving something has become scientific. The predominating desire for evidence in 'black and white' has led me to wonder if there may be a trepidation in trusting other than what the physical senses confirm as facts; perhaps a fear of the more subtle senses, which are unfamiliar to the logical mind? Intellect or the faculty of mind fears deception, though this should not cause the total banning of more subtle and ethereal skills! Humans seeking deeper levels of awareness may nevertheless remain attached to security in the form of logic and familiarity, which very often stems from an idea that it has to be one or the other. Neither intellect nor perception need exclusively dominate in our consciousness, or need be ostracized. To feel complete in our heart, mind and body - an integration and balance of both is vital. The mind with its logic is a functional mechanism of the body in an overall representation, and yet perception is precious beyond words. In my fairy realm higher intelligence is seen as the skill to see and hear beyond any limitations of physical capability.

Why not include both intellect as well as perception and fear neither?

Flowing like a river there are numerous meridians where unseen energy is routed through our physical and non-physical body. Some Western people seeking to know the Eastern ways have discovered seven energy centers in the body and named them chakras. The higher frequency tones are located in the upper region, for example the throat chakra, whereas the deeper tones are to be found in the lower parts such as the solar plexus region. The sounds of trees and rocks match the deepest chakra tones. Their mighty voices are profoundly haunting in the most exquisite way. Understanding this powerful resonance, monks living in monasteries in Tibet have integrated it into their own voices as meditation

Trees and rocks appear stationary in the physical realm, but reaching beyond such an assumption will bring about the ability to see them moving in their slow, graceful unwavering steps. They move; they have mobility! A message they have been bringing to this world for hundreds of years is to ask humans not to be confined by mere concepts. It can be a difficult task when the brain relays messages that limit a deeper comprehension. Clearly some humans find themselves confused in abstraction when they leap inadvertently into expanded knowledge, because they may not have the ability to bring such information back into the world. Einstein, a very gifted human who understood the confines of the brain, deftly stepped out of those limitations without getting lost in abstraction because he was also anchored, but not imprisoned in logic. He was gifted in transforming knowledge into substance.

PROGRESS

Progress has evolved as a goal here, which is often a presumed improvement on nature. It's understandable that the human mind in all its enthusiasm craves advancement, challenge, aspiration and development; I have never understood though, the conscious choice to destroy rather than work with nature. Development here often involves destruction of trees as well as disfigurement of rocks, while awareness of the natural place they occupy on this planet was hardly considered. This eradication of trees has been mainly for greed and personal gain, which are seen as worthwhile aspirations.

Trees and rocks look upon humans without any 'judgment' - they hold no grudges. Human are considered to be 'young ones' who are on a path towards recognizing the authentic meaning of wisdom. Trees and rocks are attempting to bring guidance on this path of evolvement.

Increasing earthly possessions is a craving in this world; perhaps this is yet another concept of attaining serenity. The falsity of such an illusion eventually becomes apparent and at some point in some lifetime it is recognized that real peace is found within. The trees and rocks wait patiently and lovingly for this recognition.

The earth exists in a delicate balance, created as a harmonic orchestra, which has been thrust into chaos. In response, trees are moving away and into other dimensions while mankind continues to ignore one of life's greatest gifts. Strange weather changes are manifesting throughout the planet, overwhelming pollution and other dramatic characteristics of imbalance are obvious. The earth's body is sick. The earth's energy chakras are congested.

Since life itself exists in balance, there is a naturally occurring consequence to every action. People in authority have contributed to an environment that will fit their own immediate needs, developing a world to suit profitable desires without taking into consideration the needs of a planet that nurtures and provides for them. When avarice takes precedence, a nurturing quality to life will be replaced by grasping. A world depleted of all its resources will no longer be able to sustain life.

There was a time when respect and gratitude towards nature was seen as a priority. Deeply embedded in their heart was the knowledge and wisdom of Native Americans who indeed demonstrated this deference; sadly they were ignored and eliminated by others who embodied different values. Choices made by humans at that time began unsettling the whole planet. Elder fairies looked upon this dimension with concern and found it necessary to communicate this issue to others from differing realms.

Greed is a wounding outcome of the mind's desire and often results in cruelty. Desperation for personal gain inevitably creates misery and loneliness. The trees and rocks offered to bring their insight into this dimension as the world was evolving. Sadly in this era of earth time they are now departing very quickly. The only reason they are leaving is that the situation created, has caused them to do so. They are not acting on reactive emotion, they simply live in balance. Annihilation is causing their departure because all action creates consequences.

Fairies are taught to honor the tree realm and would not enter their plane of existence without invitation. The wiser fairies will visit other dimensions and return with greater vision, because they are capable of receiving messages that such dimensions offer. The realm of rocks is even deeper, only the very oldest and wisest fairies enter there. On their return the elder fairies will first go into a form of hibernation so as to process the fresh information; it requires conscientious translation before it can be shared. We feel it is essential to ensure that the message is relayed in its purest form. A fairy's body becomes weighed down with this new knowledge; therefore a hibernation period serves to re-align the energy meridians. The translated information can then be freely available.

Guidance, which comes to the earth plane from a higher source, can often be misunderstood and corrupted when it is being communicated to others; this is due to the reluctance of humans to undergo a meditative time in order to process a message and thereby transmit it in an unadulterated way. Impatience in humans' causes an impulse to relay information before it's ripe. Various spiritual teachers have come to the earth and attempted to share important messages but it is clear that over the span of centuries some confusion has occurred in the translation.

On this earthly plane I am immeasurably enriched when looking at trees. While gazing at their manifold physical forms, I'm immersed in a poignant melody of silence, grace and synchronization – gratitude overflows as sacred tears flow silently down my cheeks, a bodily expression for something that cannot be said, only felt. Trees can remain on this planet for hundreds of years. They are simply here, and this presence has no time attached to it as long as humans choose to live in balance. To honor trees and rocks and to regard their appearance here with respect is of great relevance. I find it extraordinary that the most seemingly hidden and difficult treasure to find is just waiting to be seen, right there in front us! Vision and courage are necessary to seek and find this treasure. It is surely a paradox of life's teaching to finally realize that recognition of basic simplicity is all that's required in this profound act of searching.

Just as I am a fairy within a human body, beings from the tree dimension are also here in human form, though the entire reason for their appearance is yet unknown to me; I nevertheless acknowledge and value their monumental presence; verbal or physical recognition seems uncalled for. Some ideas I have shared with you will equip you to be aware of them too - even in their human form. They don't have any particular physical attributes, in fact their form can be extremely varied as well as mystifying, but their presence is unmistakable. To be guided by mere physical appearance can be misleading and confusing; many tree beings are missed by doing that.

Although the reasons for tree beings to be here in human form are unknown to me, I sense that this planet is ready for a new beginning and a different direction. I sense similar feelings in the hearts of many who perceive the true presence and significance of trees and rocks.

We are all here as part of an awe-inspiring 'painting', each color and each nuance creates the whole picture. It is only the concept of separation that creates false ideas of division. When division is felt, then the empty shell of aloneness weighs like a dark cloud on the soul. From this dark cloud of lost innocence springs the idea of grasping and greed. Subatomic particles can exist in different places at the same time and this applies to all of reality. While humans live in a three-dimensional world now, this will soon change as the discovery of new dimensions approach a conscious understanding.

Sitting under a tree will awaken you. If ever you feel despondent or uneasy with life, look towards the trees and rocks for comfort and compassion. Leaning on a rock will remind you of your strength, and give you strength. Deep solace is offered and available from trees and rocks; we have much to learn from them. The journey in human form is less hostile when you feel alive and whole and realize that you are not alone.

When you feel hurt by the cutting attacks or spite of others, by giving energy to these assaults you may be ensnared and it becomes your own burden. There are shadows too in this human world, and I have found it preferable not to fight the shadow lands or even engage in the 'crusade' or battle with sinister individuals. Pay no attention to the dark shadows of hatred, jealousy, fear and aggression because by ignoring them, it will cause them to shrivel, withdraw and evaporate; by giving your energy and focus to the enlightened path or 'the high road', it will strengthen the brightness in your own heart. It is impossible to deny the existence of duality, which is seen, as 'good and evil' existing in the world – but it is truly a choice whether or not to be pulled into the abyss of spiritual destitution where emotions of aggression, hatred and anger run rampant. Wandering away from the life-giving forest of trees and into the comatose quagmire of muddy swamps will make it very difficult to walk, run, skip or dance. Strength and commitment are required to free oneself from the swampy ground once one has entered there. It is better not to go there in the first place.

Trees and rocks offer much-needed comfort to mortals whose hurt and pain is a wound that can potentially become a deep scar, or else it can grow to be compassion and forgiveness. The connection to a divine and inner strength is revived in this healing transformation.

Houses

"The universe is full of magical things,
patiently waiting for our wits to grow sharper."

~ Eden Phillpotts

Living in square concrete rooms has been an odd experience. To a fairy, any structure with corners seems to end abruptly with a jerk; that is why I'm very comfortable in circular rooms where a sense of harmony is never-ending. Waking up within closed angular walls stifled me for a while - it seemed so rigid. To see birds', trees, sky, and the rising sun - the vision of nature and life itself are very important to me when waking in the morning. Likewise I yearn for the nightly appearance of a radiant moon shining peacefully into the room while I sleep at night - always unique and each time new, as are the myriads of stars sparkling and twinkling in the night sky. I soon found ways to be near open windows while sleeping! Ah, what bliss!

In spite of my aversion to being confined within closed walls, I realized that the human body needs protection against elements, which is provided by the houses we live in. It was a happy discovery to see skylights incorporated in homes and many buildings are now being designed so that light comes pouring in through huge windows. Some dwellings are even being built as spheres or spirals, though this is still quite rare.

Falling into a deep and silent slumber, a fairy's sleep time is very restful in circular rooms filled with copious silky walls that are composed of a transparent fabric where opaque colors are

95

intertwined with rippling rainbow tinges. They are like clear quartz crystals that are found in the rocks here when the sun is shining all the way through them and you can see radiant rainbow colors flickering from the depths, as though from some far off land. This resemblance I have made to crystals is not a perfect comparison because our walls are softer than the silkiest material. I have tried very hard to find this fabric here but alas, it cannot be anchored on the earth plane, and it simply disappears like water falling through your hand. I did come close to finding it one early morning when I was high up in the mountains. The morning dew sparkled on a single blue and white flower petal - the combination of these two elements seemed to merge in that moment to form a material I recognized. When I eagerly reached to hold it in my human hand the dew had already vanished. A complete merging of petal and dew did not occur as it does in the fairy dimension. I was suddenly overwhelmed by sad nostalgia. Falling into the soft grass I cried and cried until the gentle hand of a fairy touched my shoulder. This tender sign of comfort and compassion radiated through me and I knew I was not alone. Walking quietly away with a trusting heart, I continued my journey as a human.

Where there is a lack of trees and flowers in cities, I find myself longing to be amongst vibrant life again.

Humans seem very industrious, constructing huge structures within ever expanding cities while taking over more and more countryside. It revolves around the accumulation of wealth. Once these massive buildings are completed, people seem busy inside with telephones, pens and machines. I've yet to see the deeper value to this enterprising behavior, but I'm still new here and sincerely willing to explore ways with which to expand my viewpoint.

Are cities felt to be important in maintaining physical life and survival?

It is in effect not necessary to oppose the true nature of being in order to maintain survival of the body, and on a very intrinsic level most people do understand this – but a difficulty has arisen and a resulting fear is expressed. To truly and totally embrace this law of nature and thus live in trust and unity seems difficult for most people to attain. Fear of survival seems strong here and truth can frequently be sacrificed for the sake of this idea.

It really is possible to live in harmony with others, harmony with oneself and with the earth; it is also possible to embrace wealth and riches, by retaining the heart of unity. Sadly many people, who have accumulated wealth, seem fearful of losing it; their bodies become tense, on guard and suspicious.

Great trust is required to overcome the iron grip of fear and to celebrate whatever form our riches become visible

"Gracefulness is an outward expression
Of the inner harmony
Within our soul"

W. Hazlitt

Religion

If our religion is based on salvation,
our chief emotions will be fear and trembling.
If our religion is based on wonder,
our chief emotion will be gratitude.

—Carl Jung

In this dimension, numerous religions involve honoring a higher power - worship and devotion is felt to be sacred.

With intricate and creative designs, it is obvious that a lot of loving care has been put into constructing buildings of worship. I love the feeling of sanctity in a holy place, like a church or temple or place of pilgrimage. The quiet stillness within these monuments evokes a deep respect within people - though I am puzzled when this deference ends abruptly outside the holy edifice. Reverence for the sanctity of nature's surroundings is not so widespread, though clearly God's kingdom too. Perhaps the sanctity of nature is not obvious because it is not man-made. I can't see any separation or reason to value one place of sacredness more than another.

I feel so much joy at the reverence shown and orientated toward a divine presence of love without demanding any scientific proof of this unseen heavenly presence. In this particular instance most humans seem very trusting. Perhaps the reason for this is a conditioned ingrained doctrine or sadly, a manipulated power by some unscrupulous representatives of a belief system. Or this may even be our inherent DNA coding that requires the compliance of a 'following'. Our profound human need to feel supported and even guided is deeply ingrained and vital too.

Religions of differing 'Gods' or teachers often go to war against each other, justifying this hostility with arguments that have never made any sense to me. It seems each religion wants to prove that their own belief is the 'right' one.

I wonder if the original teachers would have sanctioned aggression in this way. Or has the information been adjusted over countless centuries since the teacher's death? After exploring different holy teachings I found beauty in all of them no matter 'which God' is honored. While there is a supportive attitude towards others in the same group, I am puzzled at the ferocious antagonism displayed between groups, the outcome of which is not so peaceful!

We don't perceive the idea of followings as being helpful; instead we encourage the total and inimitable evolvement of every individual, recognizing each as special. I mention this in view of the pattern humans have indicated by seeking as well as following a teaching, while in the process abandoning their own unique and unknown path. I believe that a teacher can point to a window – but it is up to each individual to see the window and look beyond.

After studying different creeds, my understanding is that each authentic teacher has found the pure experience of love and truth and then shared it. I cannot recall any mention of competitiveness within the original teachings. Such competition appears to have emerged after the teacher has left this earth, which makes one feel uneasy in accepting as true, the mixed and ambiguous interpretations given over the centuries to the original teachings. These middlemen or representatives may have ulterior motives, seeking self-assurance and power through instilling fear into the submissive and more compliant members of the human race. The authentic teachers are not seeking recognition or power; they are simply sharing something as though it were a poem or a song so that others too may experience this blessing. Following a spiritual path, seeking the radiance of love and peace - does not denote being meekly acquiescent!

We fairies do not have a creed where a personified God or teacher is worshipped. We see the very existence of life as sacred: plants, sky, sun, moon and every life form created, including humans and fairies - all are blessed. This certainly includes rocks as well as the whole spectrum of nature. Godliness is all encompassing in our world.

Trusting in each moment as it unfolds - our approach is to honor the mystery of life. We don't have a teaching or even a belief system we simply live life as it is being presented. This is our truth. We see this as a revered state of being.

There is a trend here to follow the latest or updated teachings; some are innovative ways of communicating newly conceptualized wisdom while others are updated versions of the original teaching. New followings emerge as a result and these are often attacked by the older more traditional versions. The competition!

After visiting a spiritual teacher in Lucknow India whose name was Poonjaji, my own experience of discovering his authentic reluctance to establish any form of organization or religion was comforting, even though this seemed to be the well-intentioned desire of many 'devotees'. This man showered immeasurable compassion on all those who came to sit and hear him speak. I understood without a doubt that he was a rock being, who in that very moment illuminated the room and myself with his presence. Immense gratitude filled my spirit as I recognized a very ancient and wise soul embodied in this eighty three year old body. His presence here on this planet was a gift of love. A few years later I miraculously found myself once again in Lucknow, where I again met the strong piercing stare of his brown eyes. He died at age eighty-seven that year.

Meditation forms part of a religion too for some people. I appreciate the company of meditators, where a golden quality of timeless emptiness pervades the room. Quiet stillness characterized by this state resonates with my fairy world. Many people who discovered the benefits of meditating for an hour or so daily have also understood the powerful and transformative effect it has on their energy. An hourly session though, is really a technique to practice meditation in order for it to become part of each minute and each second of living. True and lasting meditation is a state of being, to be lived fully all the time. Eating, shopping, exercising and indeed every single activity can be a meditation. Great awareness and presence is required. Though many even see this as a struggle or a challenge to conquer and a goal to accomplish; I see people trying hard to 'get it right' or to develop the 'correct technique' while striving and even toiling arduously for attainment and perfection.

In reality freedom is already within us all, simply waiting to be realized and fulfilled. The very nature and essence of being is already there. Perfection is to be found in imperfection; in imperfection we are perfect.

Many religions embrace the seeds of guidance and love. The mistaken and manipulated versions have made humanity fearful as well as violent, which cannot be the message originally given to this world?

I would like to put forward the suggestion that mankind follows and listens wisely to his or her own heart. It may feel unfamiliar, but your heart will speak the truth. Listen astutely and you can hear.

"No need for temples
No need for complicated philosophies,
My heart is the temple,
My philosophy is kindness"

Dalai Lama

Age and Ageing

"The fey wonders of the world only exist while there are those with the sight to see them"

~Charles de Lin

Great honor is bestowed as we age in our fairy world. Ageing is a manifestation of becoming wiser and more enlightened. Seen as a flowing and natural progression, the full and unquestionable meaning of the word beauty in connection with our ageing process - can be illustrated by a philosophical phrase: 'Beauty is in the eye of the beholder'. Fairy eyes see inner beauty very distinctly because our vision is linked closely with our heart. I am not sure how clearly these human eyes are capable of detecting inner beauty because human eyes are physically constructed to see the outer shell. I believe being attentive on deeper levels enables one to see and feel the glow of another person – internal radiance is unmistakable and this can be seen through human eyes.

'Growing old' seems terrifying to some people and a desire to remain young instigates strong resistance to the natural outcome of living in a body. Ideas of ugliness or beauty in this dimension are often related to physical appearance, thus ageing is not considered to be beautiful whereas youth is. Age is sometimes seen as repugnant, even thought to repel love. Men and women have become somewhat accustomed to falling in love with an exterior facade. Sadly the innocence of love is manipulated by such concepts; nobody wants to be denied the experience of love so they will strive to force their physical appearance into the 'right mould' - it is a continual activity here causing tension and struggle. The 'right mould' seems to depend on the mood of the times!

It took me a long time to comprehend that this behavior results from so much value being placed on the outer shell. People decorate themselves with obvious motive and intensity using cosmetics, jewelry and fashionable clothes. This very effort when somberly invested in the act of embellishment can cause hard tension lines. On the other hand playfully adorning the body while enjoying the experience demands no pressure and results in softer lines! Many people forcing themselves into a mould in order to be worthy of love will suffer tremendous anxiety and pain. It is a boundless dilemma unless one steps out of the iron grip of this thought pattern.

Giving and receiving love is really a natural expression of every being, which cannot be programmed or manipulated into conditions dependent on physical appearance alone; attempting to do so is likely to cause a profound misunderstanding of the true experience of loving. Wanting and being wanted are often mistaken for loving. Desire is mistaken for love.

Children and elderly people generally seem less attached to the physical expressions of being 'beautiful or ugly'. They have a tendency to see beyond superficial labeling – appreciating inner beauty as the authentic element. Untainted by judgments, there is a natural companionship among these two generations, the common ground being a spark of innocence and the ability to bring true loving into relating.

It is characteristic of many though, to reject their own appearance and thus become obsessed with changing it. People resort to plastic surgery more and more. It is truly wonderful to experience the benefits of technology as mankind discovers deeper aspects to scientific knowledge. Plastic surgery, a fascinating topic of exploration and pioneering, has been known to heal badly damaged facial wounds and it has proven to be exceptionally restorative. But to criticize and reject one's own naturally unique physical form, only serves to encourage and deepen the despair of mankind. The failure to love who you are as you are, may further intensify the use of quick and easy ways to 'change' your body and even your mind.

"In order to love who you are,
you cannot hate the experiences
that shaped you"

Andrea Dykstra

The true and indisputable nature of a body involves the ageing process. I am experiencing this myself, and see the gentle way and sometimes not so gentle way, my corporal body moves from youth to maturity. Even though I view my physical form as I would a set of clothes, very temporary, I do experience times when I would most certainly wish for a youthful body again. A fantasy! Clinging to preserve it by fighting nature is most certainly inducing a struggle and a losing battle! I wonder if such clinging is motivated by feelings in some, that they haven't lived a full life? I am not even sure that I have lived my own life fully when looking back at decisions and opportunities I may have missed or expressed differently; but after all musings and analyzing, I can say that my life is being lived and I honor that. We all go through questions and feelings, wondering whether we made the 'right' decisions – looking back on our life there are numerous potential and alternative choices. Wisdom and peace will finally impart the truth that this is the path we ultimately chose. What is there to chastise or to change from the past? Walking onward with dignity, with love and with peace is to release the past and to live fully now in the moment, even with an ageing body!

Treating a body with the same respect as one would a temple is in itself a form of honoring nature. I have seen a recklessness expressed by a few people towards their ageing body, thus encouraging its breakdown. Is this a desperate attempt to free their inner being, even though it ultimately creates more shackles? The turning point between true freedom and being further shackled is very subtle – I believe that a willingness to allow rather than struggle against life's teachings is the essence of freedom we so long for.

Have compassion for the life you have lived and the life that you are now living. It is a gift. The body ages! I want to remind humans, and this also serves to remind myself, that our essence is more than a just a body!

Wear purple and red colors! Ride a bicycle in your eighties – celebrate your life whatever age you are. Let go of regret and begin your journey as a new day – everyday.

Laugh, cry, love and LIVE!

"Dancers are the messengers of the Gods"

~Martha Graham

Death and Dying

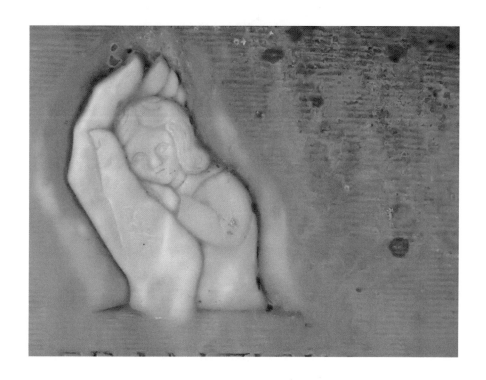

"Only when you have drunk

from the river of silence

Shall you indeed truly sing"

Kahlil Gibran

A deep attachment to the body has brought about a sense of foreboding surrounding the aspect of death; it's become 'important' to cling on to the physical form. The bodily functions will undoubtedly shut down when it's time, but your true being can never die. A physical body is the vehicle used to experience the earth dimension for a specific duration of time.

Death is treated as a solemn issue in this realm and I empathize so very deeply with this response, yet at the same time knowing there *is* an illusion created by such a phenomenon. Those who have actually seen a dead body will recognize that the spark of life has moved on and there is now an empty shell. We shed tears of grief for the loss of that sparkle of life, so dear to us, that was manifested through the corporal body of someone we have known – though it's clear that the life force *has* moved elsewhere. The body returns to the earth where it came from. The spirit is re-born into consciousness.

Some humans fight the physical process of departure as though it were a terrible enemy; panic and fear arise in this challenge for *survival* – it becomes a battle for existence! 'Fighting' for life gracefully – with all the vivacity and humility of sincere passion, is exceptionally beautiful; but fighting for life with a grasping and wrenching desire to be in control can only bring distress. Where there *is* a possibility for healing, the 'fight' takes on a different dynamic. There are known situations where a person's health has declined so much that recovery seems impossible, and yet miraculously a resurgence of new life takes place. Prayers and hopes of all those around a sick person can and does create an energy field of healing – it's called a miracle. A concentration of heartfelt thoughts generates a vibrational field that works in ways still mysterious to mankind; it is a phenomenon of science that has not yet been clearly identified. The power of prayer does not emerge from control but from pure love. Sudden and irrational revival can be an unfathomable mystery as in the miraculous recovery of certain individuals who were presumed to be ready for death. It is Grace.

Life threatening diseases although declared incurable may inexplicably leave the body, which is a mystery to logic and science! Even though science may claim *no hope* in some cases, it still may *not* be the rightful time to leave. To simply relinquish bodily life based on a foundation of mere words is unwise and choosing to avoid, escape or reject life by abandoning the bodily form through self-destruction will not and cannot bring liberation. To neither give up nor cling, is a paradox which only makes sense when the heart is open to love. Many will know that people have recovered from terminal illness and others who have desperately wished to relinquish their life, have nonetheless remained. It is Grace.

The natural movement of life involves death. Those who truly value life don't fear death because to fear life is to fear death too. Trepidation of the ambiguity surrounding death can mount up and fill the body with anxiety as well as suffering. It's the human state of affairs to feel apprehension towards these countless *and* unknown aspects of our lives.

This 'dying' process brings with it the capacity to have a tremendously illuminating experience as one moves from the physical to the non-physical dimensions. The body and soul separate again and it is revealed in full consciousness how at birth, the body and soul came together for a certain length of time.

When experiencing this transition one may be reminded of the changing seasons within this earth plane, each season is unique and splendid. One's heart and soul encounters a new beginning as a season ends and a new one is set in motion. *Death* of summer brings with it the *birth* of autumn; *death* of winter brings the *birth* of spring. Once the body has been left behind on this earth realm, it is apparent that the 'new season' is another dimension filled with enlightenment. A new season! Any of life's changes, when met with courage and recognition brings about a deep receptivity of the heart.

It is a sad time for those who must say goodbye to a beloved one. It's difficult to let go. My own personal confrontation of being in this body and seeing my baby daughter, my mother and then my father die has been exceedingly sad. The sadness touched my being profoundly, yet at times, I saw in my sorrow another feature to experience within this form I have taken, which is to acknowledge the transient and illusory nature of a material plane. I feel the presence of my daughter and parents, even though they may not be seen in physical form.

A writer by the name of Stephen Levine touched my heart with his written words: *'When it is deeply understood that nothing is permanent, then wisdom grows'*. He spoke of death and the precious gift of providing a quiet sanctuary for a person to leave in peace and acceptance. By sitting quietly and lovingly beside someone who is going through the dying process, is giving this person time as well as the space to depart with serenity and understanding. I have found this compassionate and loving approach to be of great value within the hospice movements.

Since fairies are not confined in the physical plane, we see death as a manifestation of change. Fairies don't experience death as it's seen here; we recognize infinity and eternity. Within this recognition, there are always *changes* to go through. We don't look into the future because *future* is not an issue of concern in our sphere of understanding. We do allow our life to unfold from moment-to-moment; each moment being so complete that death as perceived here, does not exist. Only the moment exists. In our world, changes are encountered and confronted as they arise - one such change can be labeled as death.

Living 'in the moment' may be misunderstood as recklessness here. Clearly, practical matters on earth do entail some attention to future matters. There are considerations involving upcoming events, which require thoughtful awareness – yet 'living in the moment' does not call for the abandonment of responsibility. Seeing beyond this physical form and into the eternity of freedom can be difficult when obstructed by tension and even too much 'logic'. I also know that to live in the world one must embrace and integrate both the spiritual *and* the physical as a universal energy force.

I am awaiting further information on this subject and will share it as soon as becomes a clear manifestation. Trees and rocks can and *do* offer insightful knowledge; reaching out and embracing their wisdom will deepen human understanding.

Life in this mortal form is essential for discernment to take place. Don't imagine that by jumping off a cliff you will find illumination, the lifespan allocated to each human has a specific path for a meaningful journey.

Death is not to be feared, nor need it be sort after as a means of escaping life. Existence is a mystery far more expansive than the reasoning or mortal mind – there are people who have experienced an authentic *near-death-experience,* and returned to quietly share this valuable knowledge.

Time

"The only reason for time
Is so that everything
Doesn't happen at once"

Albert Einstein

Since Einstein's theory of relativity in 1905,
we know that time can speed up, slow down, warp and bend.
Time travel is possible when we consider space travel
and our evolving understanding of astro physics.
The technology is possible to allow people from different times to
communicate, through a 'time phone'.
Scientists search for the Higgs singlet, a sub atomic particle believed
to be able to travel through time dimensions.
The large Hadron Collider (LHC) is. the world's largest and most
powerful particle collider and is in Switzerland.

Fairies recognize the existence of time in a realm where this configuration has been established and must exist on specific levels of understanding. The structure of time has been ingeniously developed on this earth plane because living in time is necessary – a concept and reality in this dimension. Matter moves forward 'in time', whereas anti-matter travels backwards 'in time'.

By living in the 'now', it is actually possible to reach moments of timelessness within this worldly configuration. Being completely focused on whatever the moment brings and living it in its totality, is embracing timelessness. Children have this knack; their actions and words are unrehearsed and innocent. This is also a deep trust in life. This is also the portal to forms of communication other than verbal and even beyond our known universe.

Some difficulties may arise while living in time. Deadlines, postponement and the pressure to 'do' it all within a certain measurement can often generate discomfort and anxiety while feeling constricted and confined by the illusory restrictions imposed by time. Subtle yet severe judgments of this very structure often result from people feeling encumbered within the law of time. Fully discerning the more expanded levels and dimensions of consciousness, is to find peace in your life contrary to living in bondage and thinking oneself a victim of life's changes or idiosyncrasies.

Another aspect of time and often difficult to comprehend is the death of a 'young' person – a baby, a child, someone in their twenties, thirties or even forties. It seems unfair! There is a distinct feeling that this emergent life was unfairly cut short. An accident, an illness – unforeseen and unexpected. A terrible shock to all those involved. The concept of chronological age has caused much pain and anguish when relating to the death of a young person, as I myself experienced with the death of my baby daughter, Faye Claudia.

Time is relative and only measured by this physical existence, which includes the life span of each individual. A person who departs at a young age may have accomplished that very thing they came to this earth plane to experience. The quality as well as the length of a lifespan should be considered precious - it's not possible for anyone to judge the value or meaning of another's life. We can't know exactly what the purpose of each life span is meant to be.

Imagining life without time may seem perplexing to the logical mind; in order to attain true wisdom though, it is necessary to be confronted by the structure of this physical plane, to realize the necessity of certain orders governing it, and then to see beyond it. This does not suggest the rejection or denial of such rules. I've seen this very negation expressed by rebellious spirits who in defiance of the law-of-time, ardently seek to untie any restrictions placed on their freedom. A self-destructive approach obviously fails to achieve that very liberty. Achieving ultimate and original intelligence while in the body is the final realization of every being. It is 'coming home' in the truest sense.

Timelessness allows real freedom. Playful relaxation, sincerity rather than seriousness and genuine meditation are all exciting and harmonious ways with which to move into timelessness, without losing the healthy knowledge of being naturally anchored in a physical world.

Now is real. Yesterday has gone and tomorrow is not here. Only now truly exists. I once found an ancient Native American quote that voiced it in this way:

'YESTERDAY IS ASHES,
TOMORROW IS WOOD, ONLY TODAY IS FIRE! '

"The past, present and future are concepts
within the understanding of this dimension
–yet for us it is all One painting where all exist as One."

Araminta

Epilogue

"To love is human.
To feel pain is human.
Yet to still love
despite the pain
is pure Angel"

Rumi

Charmiene Maxwell-Batten

All that I've shared may not at this time be proved nor authenticated through the intellectual process. The validation lies within the spirit of us all. In human language it will be ambiguous. Proving things becomes obsolete when seeing beyond a physical realm and the physics of this dimension. Envisioning a more expansive cosmos than the limitations presented by a material, world is the supreme path of all beings in this dimension. Until then, all I have related may be interpreted as murmurings of truth, good psychology and philosophy – or perhaps just an uplifting message.

Many people have already touched upon those realms beyond intellect, thereby finding wisdom in encompassing their intuitive perception in this material plane. For those, it requires remarkable courage to trust in this foresight of truth, which is as mind-blowing as the universe. We, you and I, and all of us are in human form at this time - at any moment the possibility of seeing the absolute infinity is available.

It is a known characteristic to be forgetful once the human form is taken. I experienced this forgetfulness myself until I recognized my fairy soul. I am grateful for the beloved friends who walk with me on my journey here in the world - friends who continually remind me of wakefulness. It's easy to 'fall asleep' and forget! Waking from this allegorical sleep sounds simple, it *is* simple, and yet very multifaceted!

The truth is that we are all -

FREE, ETERNAL AND ONE!

Araminta's Message was first written in 1991 while Charmiene was walking through the primordial rocky and tree filled moorland in Haytor, England. Anyone who knows Dartmoor will recognize the enchantment of this magical and striking terrain as well as the inspiration it offers.

photo by Ritzy Ryciak

Charmiene Maxwell-Batten was born in Devon, England in the small town of Axminster. At six weeks old she left for Uganda, with her parents and Brother Jonathan. Charmiene's father was a government inspector and consultant in the coffee industry on the East African continent at the time. Charmiene and her brother lived in Kampala for ten years as the family grew; those were joyful events when Justin and Margherita were born at Entebbe hospital in Kampala and later when the family returned to England, Dominic the youngest sibling was born.

Charmiene has a profound interest in Natural health, alternative medicine, herbal remedies as well as an early and creative passion for ballet and writing, which has continued throughout her life.

Her many years in Switzerland, India, Thailand and USA have provided a deep appreciation for cultural diversity and her visits to three spiritual teachers in India have given her an understanding of our inner and human journey in this world.

In 1992 she was inspired to write and share her experiences. Charmiene's paternal great grandfather, Reverend Sabine Baring-Gould, the author of the well-known hymns *'Onward Christian Soldiers'* and *'Now the Day is Over'*, was also an avid traveler and major literary figure, who was an authority on myths, legends and folklore. Baring-Gould was a friend and literary peer of George Bernard Shaw and Arthur Conan Doyle. His marriage to Grace Taylor was the basis of the character Eliza Doolittle in Pygmalion. Rumor has it that that his estate Lew Trenchard Manor in Dartmoor, provided the atmosphere and setting for Conan Doyle's *'Hound of the Baskervilles'*. Baring Gould also appears as a character in Laurie King's Sherlock Holmes novel – *'The Moor'*.

Sabine Baring-Gould

Charmiene at Lew Trenchard Manor 1993

Charmiene by the portrait
of the young Sabine Baring-Gould and his mother

"Charmiene, the effect of your highly original work was both profound and spiritual. The night after I read 'Araminta's Message' I had a most unusual dream – a new dimension where I shed all the cumbersome load of phobias, irrational restraints and self-erected barriers and no go areas. It was light and liberating.

Your book takes me back to my first lifetime recollection when I was 2 years old and strapped in a pram in the garden. The beautiful spring morning filled me with wonderment.

You should indeed be commended for having given access to what constitutes the very antithesis of contemporary and often superficial values and viewpoints"

Frank Lyon, South Africa, January 1999

"While Charmiene Maxwell-Batten lovingly, gracefully and joyfully relays fairy Araminta's experience of this human realm, we are provided a lovely reminder of what it means to be human. The wonder and sanctity of this life, its incredible nuance, the gift of both presence and listening, and the gift of what comes from cultivating awareness, these are some of the poignant lessons that can be gleamed from this sweet tale. I found one of the most

137

empowering messages to be the importance of living with an open heart.

Collectively, the characteristics that "Minty" highlights are those that allow us to see the divinity that we are always surrounded by; they are also characteristics that help us to reach our full potential. We are reminded of the nourishment and peace that we give and receive from nature; and that healing and heartfelt joy are ways of being that we have innate access to. We are also reminded that courage can help us to overcome and be liberated from the trappings of fear. And, we can fully embrace and be empowered by the beauty of our individuality as well as being invigorated by the connectivity of the global collective - Charmiene provides her readers a warm invitation. This is an invitation to remember, awaken, and love - wholeheartedly and sincerely. I am so thankful to have been made privy to the wealth of insights found in Araminta's Message.

N. Lattanzio, California USA